Annie and Snowball and the Cozy Nest

The Fifth Book of Their Adventures

Cynthia Rylant

Illustrated by Suçie Stevenson

SIMON & SCHUSTER BOOKS FOR YOUNG READERS
New York   London   Toronto   Sydney

For my good friends:
Sarah Robinson, Lisa Markley, and Sophie
—S. S.

SIMON & SCHUSTER BOOKS FOR YOUNG READERS
An imprint of Simon & Schuster Children's Publishing Division
1230 Avenue of the Americas, New York, New York 10020
Text copyright © 2009 by Cynthia Rylant
Illustration copyright © 2009 by Suçie Stevenson
All rights reserved, including the right of reproduction
in whole or in part in any form.
SIMON & SCHUSTER BOOKS FOR YOUNG READERS
is a trademark of Simon & Schuster, Inc.
Book design by Tom Daly
The text for this book is set in Goudy.
The illustrations for this book are rendered in pen-and-ink and watercolor.
Manufactured in the United States of America
2 4 6 8 10 9 7 5 3 1
Library of Congress Cataloging-in-Publication Data
Rylant, Cynthia.
Annie and Snowball and the cozy nest / Cynthia Rylant ;
illustrated by Suçie Stevenson.—1st ed.
p. cm.
Summary: Annie and her bunny watch and wait as a nest is built
above the porch swing, and eventually they get to see the
mother bird feeding her babies.
ISBN-13: 978-1-4169-3943-6 (hardcover)
ISBN-10: 1-4169-3943-1 (hardcover)
[1. Nests—Fiction. 2. Birds—Fiction. 3. Animals—Infancy—Fiction.]
I. Stevenson, Suçie, ill. II. Title.
PZ7.R982Anc 2009
[E]—dc22
2007031056

Contents

Happy Day

It was May and Annie was happy.

So many good things were happening.

Her cousin, Henry, was having a birthday.

The tulips she planted were blooming.
And on her porch someone
was making a nest.
The nest was in a safe little spot.

Annie had seen it one day
when she was reading
with her bunny, Snowball.
"Snowball, look!" Annie had said.
"A nest!"

Annie called Henry next door and
asked him to come and see the nest.
He did.

And every day since then
Annie and Henry had hoped to see
who was building the nest.

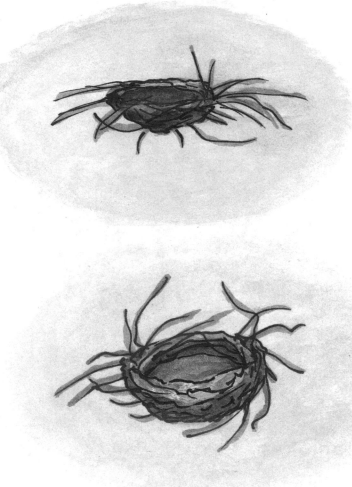

The nest was getting bigger and bigger.

Annie could see the bits of twig and
bits of leaves and even some small bits
of fur.

She wondered if it was Snowball fur.
Then she wondered if it was Mudge fur.

Henry's big dog, Mudge, had enough
extra fur to fill an elephant's nest!
(If elephants built nests.)

12

Annie checked the little nest
every day to see if anyone was home.
But so far no one had moved in.

A New Neighbor

One day Annie was reading
on the swing when a little robin
swooped above her head.
The swoop made Snowball jump.

Annie looked up at the nest.
Someone was home!
It was the little robin!

Annie watched quietly as the little
robin settled into her cozy home.
The nest was in a perfect place to
hatch babies.

A person would never know the nest
was there unless he sat on Annie's
swing.

And no one sat on Annie's swing
except Annie and Snowball and
sometimes Henry and sometimes
Annie's dad.

17

Mudge did not sit on Annie's swing.
(Though sometimes he tried.)

The little robin and the little nest
were perfectly safe.
Annie had a new neighbor!

Waiting and Waiting

For days and days Annie quietly watched
the little robin sit in its cozy nest.
The little bird was almost always there.

When it flew away, Annie worried that
it might not come back.
But it always did.
And Annie knew why.

One day when the bird was away, Annie's dad lifted her up to look inside the nest.

"Five eggs!" whispered Annie.
"Five blue eggs!"

Annie's dad told her she could look at
the eggs but not to touch them.

He said that mother birds do not like
fingers touching their eggs.
So Annie did not touch.

She wanted the little robin to be happy
living on the porch.
Henry and his dad came over to see
the eggs too.

"Five eggs," said Henry's dad. "She's
hatching a basketball team."

Annie and Henry laughed.

Henry's dad could be so silly.

Everyone could hardly wait to see the
babies.

A Family

The baby birds picked the perfect
morning to hatch.
It was a Saturday morning.

Annie and Annie's dad and Henry
and Henry's dad and Henry's mom
and Snowball and Mudge were all
in Annie's kitchen having pancakes.

(Snowball loved lettuce pancakes.)

The doors were open. The windows were open.
And somehow everyone was chewing at the same time, so it was quiet.
Then suddenly . . . *cheep cheep cheep cheep cheep*!

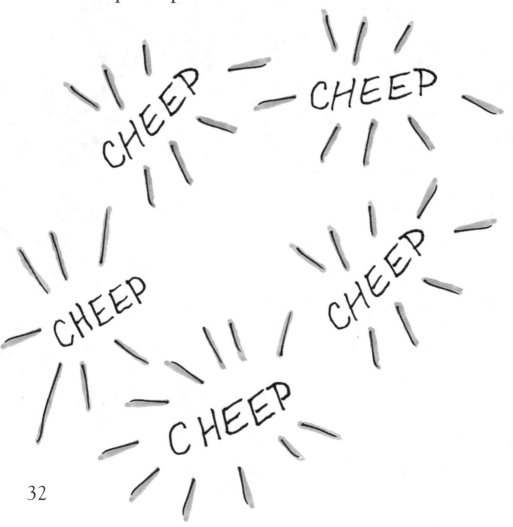

The sounds came from the front porch!
And they were loud!

Annie's dad said, "I think someone else
wants breakfast!"
Everyone hurried to the porch.

And there in the cozy nest were five
baby birds, eyes closed, mouths open,
all cheeping.

The little robin was perched on the
nest, putting bits of food in each
baby's mouth.
"They're beautiful!" said Annie.
"And really hungry!" said Henry.

Mudge's ears were perked up.
Cheeping was a new sound to him.

"I'm proud of the mother," said Annie.
"She waited and waited and waited."
When the last baby was fed, the little
robin flew off to find more food.

"That reminds me," said Henry.
"Pancakes!" said Henry and Annie
together.

They all went back inside to the table.
Then everyone was chewing *and* talking.
It had been an exciting morning.
The excitement had made them hungrier.

While everyone ate, Mudge and
Snowball curled up under the table.

"Look," said Annie. "Snowball has her own cozy nest."
"Yes," said Henry, "but this nest snores!"